GNOCCHI
Italy

GYOZA
Japan

MANTOO
Afghanistan

MOMO
Nepal

KNAIDEL
Central & Eastern Europe

SHUMAI
China

TORTELLINI
Italy

CHOCHOYOTE
Mexico

PIEROGI
Poland

FUFU
Ghana

RAVIOLI
Italy

KNAIDEL
k'NAY-del

CHOCHOYOTE
cho-cho-YO-teh

FUFU
foo-foo

MOMO
mo-mo

MANTOO
mahn-TOO

GYOZA
g'YO-zah

SHUMAI
shoo-my

RAVIOLI
ra-vee-OH-lee

TORTELLINI
tor-teh-LEE-nee

GNOCCHI
n'YO-kee

PIEROGI
pih-ROHG-ee

© 2021 Sunbird Books, an imprint of Phoenix International Publications, Inc.
8501 West Higgins Road   59 Gloucester Place
Chicago, Illinois 60631   London W1U 8JJ

www.sunbirdkidsbooks.com

Library of Congress Control Number: 2020943566

ISBN: 978-1-5037-5710-3 Printed in China

The art for this book was created digitally while eating dumplings.
Cover design and typography by Andrea Fronc. Text set in **Gilroy** and LEMON YELLOW SUN.

LiTTLE DUMPLiNGS

Written by Susan Rich Brooke
Illustrated by Bonnie Pang

sunbird books

SPLiSH, **SPLASH**, SPLiSH!

The Little Dumpling happily paddled through the salty broth, over the onions, around the carrots, and through the leafy dill. "Stop making waves," her sister complained.

The Little Dumpling smiled and listened to the sound of the dumpling chef **PATTiNG** the dough.

PAT, **PAT**, PAT...

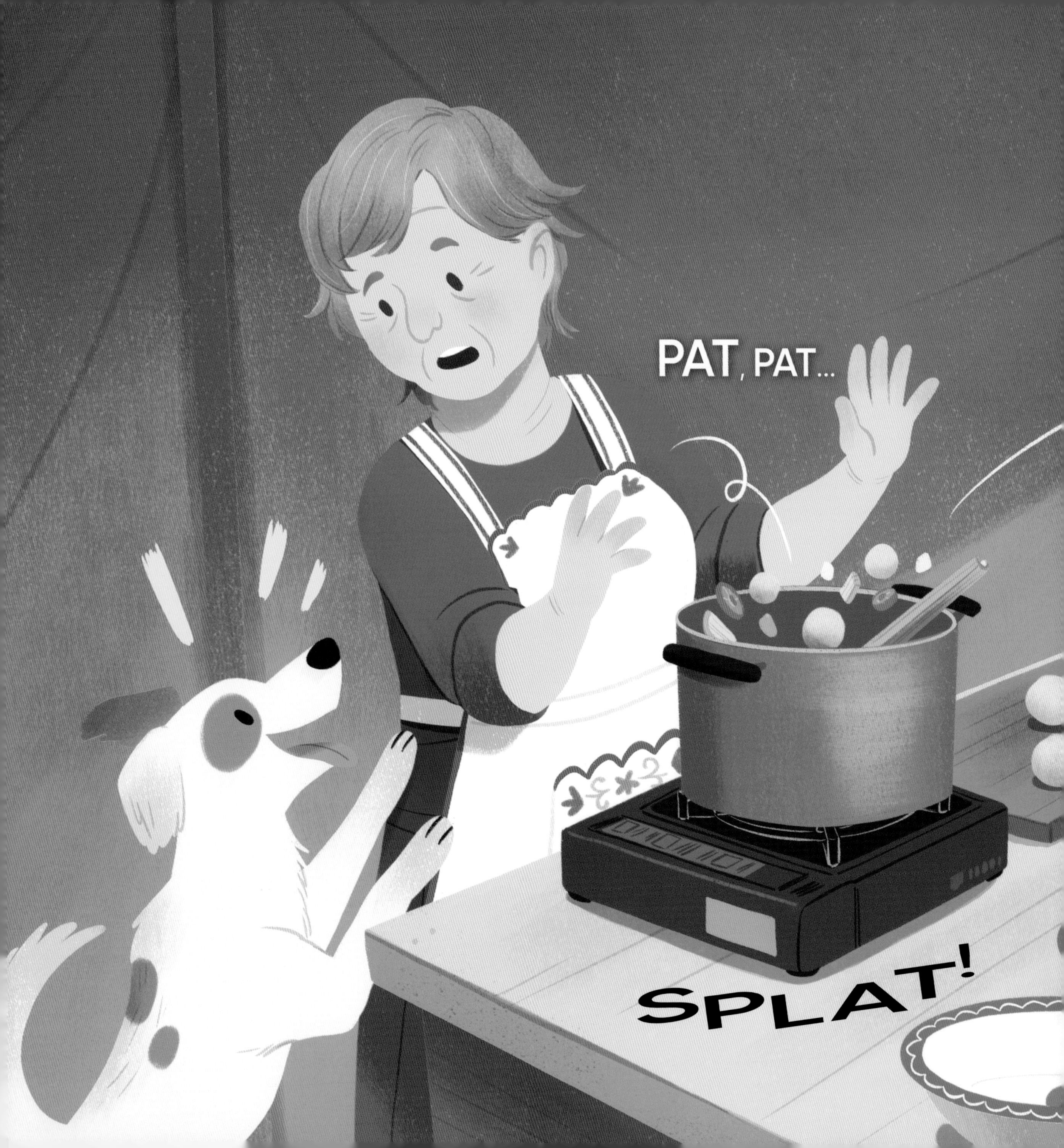
PAT, PAT...
SPLAT!

WHOOOOOOOOOOA!

The Little Dumpling tumbled and twisted, head over heels, far, far away from the big pot of salty broth that she called home. It might have been fun...if it weren't so frightening.

When she finally rolled to a stop, the Little Dumpling stood up and looked around.

Where in the world...?!?

OK. She was at something called a "Dumpling Fest."

All she needed to do was find her tent...out of the dozens and dozens of tents.

Oh, and get away from that dog.

At the edge of a tent, the Little Dumpling spotted a familiar shape. "Excuse me," she called. "Could you help me..."

The creature was round like a dumpling. But he had a big dent right in the middle of his head!

"I'm fine, thanks," he said. "Hello, I'm **CHOCHOYOTE**."

"Hi, I'm Little Dumpling!"

CHOCHOYOTE laughed. "We're all little dumplings here."

"You seem lost," **CHOCHOYOTE** said. "But I think I know where you might be from." He led the Little Dumpling to the tent next door and said, "Meet my friend **FUFU**."

FUFU was round like the Little Dumpling, but she was lighter in color, a bit bigger, and less bumpy.

"Someone's coming!" said **FUFU**. "Quick, dive into the stew!"

WHOOOSH!

Well. This wasn't a salty broth. It was warm, but it was thick and chunky, and the Little Dumpling had never felt, or smelled, anything like it. When no one was looking, she took a tiny taste. It was different...and delicious!

"Thanks for hiding me," the Little Dumpling said to **FUFU**.
"But I'd better head home."

Along the row of tents, she met **MOMO**, who also called herself a dumpling. She had a filling on the inside, and she was pinched closed in a pretty pattern.

And she met **MANTOO**, who was filled and pinched AND covered in sauce.

She met **GYOZA**, who was filled and folded and fried in a pan.

And she met **SHUMAi**, who was open at the top!

I LIKE THE BREEZE!

PATTED, PiNCHED, FiLLED, FOLDED, POACHED, PAN-FRIED, STEAMED, SAUCED!
The Little Dumpling had no idea there were so many different ways to be a dumpling!

"Hello, I'm **RAVIOLI**," said the rectangular dumpling at the next tent. "These are my cousins, **TORTELLINI** and **GNOCCHI**."

"Dog!" shouted **GNOCCHi**, diving into a white sauce. **RAVIOLi** jumped into a red sauce. **TORTELLiNi** belly-flopped into a broth, and the Little Dumpling followed her.

It was fun to swim and chat with the cousins, and the broth felt warm and good. But the Little Dumpling still missed her home.

"How long do you think that dog will hang around?" she asked.

"I have an idea," said **RAVIOLI**. "We'll form a pyramid, climb up to the shelf, and distract him with a turnip. Get ready to run!"

The Little Dumpling ran far and fast...and right into **PiEROGi!**

"Whoops!" said the crescent-shaped dumpling, who was sour-cream-topped. "Slow down and smell the dill."

"Did you say DILL?" asked the Little Dumpling.
She took a deep breath...

...and she smelled the familiar scent.

And not only that, she smelled onions...
and carrots...
and celery...

"You need a bath," her sister said. "Is that...SAUCE?"

The Little Dumpling smiled. It was good to be home. But as she paddled through the salty broth, she wondered what her new friends were doing. And she wondered if there were even more new friends to meet.

So she hugged her family...

...and went off to find out.

GYOZA
Japan

GNOCCHI
Italy

MOMO
Nepal

MANTOO
Afghanistan

TORTELLINI
Italy

KNAIDEL
Central & Eastern Europe

SHUMAI
China

CHOCHOYOTE
Mexico

PIEROGI
Poland

FUFU
Ghana

RAVIOLI
Italy